Shoot for the Moon, Robyn

Hazel Hutchins

Shoot for the Moon, Robyn

Illustrations by Yvonne Cathcart

FIRST NOVELS

The New Series

Formac Publishing Limited
Halifax, Nova Scotia

Formac Publishing Company Limited acknowledges the support of The Canada Council and the Nova Scotia Department of Education and Culture in the development of writing and publishing in Canada.

Canadian Cataloguing in Publication Data

Hutchins, H. J. (Hazel J.)

Shoot for the moon, Robyn

(First novel series)

ISBN 0-88780-388-1 (pbk.) ISBN 0-88780-389-X (bound)

I. Cathcart, Yvonne. II. Title. III. Series.

PS8565.U826S46 1997 jC813'.54 C96-950244-3
PZ7.H88Sh 1997

Formac Publishing Limited
5502 Atlantic Street
Halifax, NS B3H 1G4

Printed and bound in Canada.

Table of Contents

To Ms Scowcroft's Grade 3 class

1
Big Dreams

My name is Robyn and I'm the world's greatest singer.

Well, maybe not yet. But one day.

The songs on the Academy Awards show are what really got me interested in singing. The costumes, lights, and dancing made it all seem bigger than life. I like that.

Last week I started practising in my bedroom. It was early morning and wonderfully quiet.

"Do, re, mi, fa..."

Scales are what I practised—like in that old movie, *The*

Sound of Music. I know all about scales because I take piano lessons. With scales you don't have to know a lot of words.

"Do, re, mi, fa..."

It sounded pretty good in the quiet of my room, at least until the Kelly twins in the apartment next door started howling.

The Kelly twins are five weeks old. They look like cartoon characters—big heads and crossed eyes.

"Robyn," my mom said at breakfast. "Please don't make noise in your room in the morning. You woke up the twins."

"Those two don't need anyone to wake them up," I told my mom. "They wake up by themselves—all night long."

"I know," said my mom, "but it seems worse lately. Mr. and Mrs. Kelly look so tired. Remember how good they've always been to you—all the movies they've taken you to see? And the chocolate eggs at Easter?"

Not this Easter. This Easter I'd been replaced by the twins.

But my mom was right. I decided not to sing in my room anymore. Not even when the Kelly twins are 16 years old and blasting me out with rock music.

But I'm still going to be the world's greatest singer.

2
Spit Balls and Song

Music class at our school isn't where we do music. It's where we listen to music. Listen and draw pictures. Listen and write stories. Listen and duck spit-balls.

The Three Gs shoot the spit-balls—Grant Smith, Ari Grady, and Linden Abergeiser. Aber-geiser is stretching the "g" idea but we have to have some name for them. The teachers won't let Marie and I call them "the Three Twerps" the way we want to.

Our music teacher, Mr. Her-bert, only comes to our school

once a week. He doesn't know how to handle the Three Gs. Last Monday he put on some music, told us to draw pictures, and leaned back in his chair with his eyes closed. Talk about asking for trouble!

Spitballs began to fly. I began to duck. The Three Gs weren't even aiming at me, but I got hit—twice!

I was pretty mad, but I had more important things on my mind.

At the end of class I went to talk to Mr. Herbert.

"I think we should sing in music class," I said. "Just a suggestion."

"And a good suggestion," said Mr. Herbert, "except this isn't regular music class, it's Music

Appreciation."

"Oh," I said.

"If I'd known you liked to sing, Robyn, you could have been in choir last fall," said Mr. Herbert. "I'm sorry."

How was I supposed to know in September that in April I'd want to become a singer?

"That's okay," I said. "Anyway, I'm doing lessons on my own."

"You are?" he said. "Would you like to sing for us next week?"

There is a motto I read somewhere, or maybe I heard it on TV. It jumped into my head as Mr. Herbert stood there waiting for me to answer.

SOMETIMES YOU ONLY GET ONE CHANCE.

Just like that it jumped into my head—capital letters and all, like a billboard. Besides, next Monday was a whole week away.

"Okay," I said.

Mr. Herbert put my name down in his book just as the bell rang.

"Everyone may go—except Grant, Ari, and Linden," he said.

Maybe Mr. Herbert isn't as dozy as I thought.

As I walked out the door Grant gave me a dirty look. What was that for?

3
The Three Twerps

Marie and I went to get our jackets. I told Marie about Mr. Herbert asking me to sing.

"Because of my singing lessons," I explained.

"I thought you took piano lessons," said Marie.

"They go together," I said, which was kind of true because of me knowing about scales.

"Maybe you'll be a famous singer when you grow up," said Marie.

Marie is my best friend.

"Snitch! Tattletale! Snitch!"

Grant, Ari, and Linden were

walking up the stairs from the music room.

"Robyn the Snitch!" said Grant.

"What are you talking about?" I asked.

"We have to write essays—30 reasons why we shouldn't shoot spitballs in class," said Ari.

"All because you complained," said Linden.

"I didn't complain," I said.

"We saw you," said Ari, "just before the bell."

"I wasn't complaining. Mr. Herbert was asking me to sing for the class next week," I said.

"What a lie!" said Ari.

"Snitch!" said Linden.

"I stood beside you at the Christmas concert. You sing like a sick cow!" hooted Grant.

"Go back and ask him," I said.

"I'm not going to ask Mr. Herbert anything—not when he's just given me an essay to write," said Grant. "We'll just wait until next week. That'll prove what a snitch you are."

"Fine," I said. "Come on, Marie."

We walked down the hall and out the doors.

"I think you should sing something by Celine Dion," said Marie.

Marie is nuts about Celine Dion.

"I don't know the words to her songs," I said.

It was true. In fact I didn't know the words to many songs at all—by anybody. I could hum lots of songs in my head, but the only songs I really knew the words to were Christmas carols. Which reminded me…

"Did Grant really stand beside me at last year's Christmas concert?" I asked.

"I don't remember," said Marie, "but if Mr. Herbert asked you to sing you really must be good."

Right—kind of.

4
Baby Buggy Boogie

Marie asked me to her house to listen to Celine Dion tapes. I went home instead. I wanted to try singing—just in case.

Mrs. Kelly and the twins were trying to go into their apartment. Mrs. Kelly was searching for her keys in the bottom of her enormous purse. The twins were lying in their buggy, howling their little cartoon character lungs out.

"Are they okay?" I asked.

"Oh, Robyn, I don't know. Babies cry a lot but they've had colds and they just keep on and on," said Mrs. Kelly. "So long as I keep the buggy moving they're all right, but the minute I stop..."

The twins wailed louder. Mrs. Kelly scrabbled frantically in her purse. I decided to experiment. I pushed the buggy a little way down the hall. The howling quietened down. I pushed the buggy further down the hall. The howling stopped. I pushed the buggy all the way to the end of the hall and pulled it all the way back. Mrs. Kelly had the door open.

"I could push it a little longer," I said. I wanted to see how long the experiment would work.

"Would you, Robyn?" asked Mrs. Kelly. "Just until I get a

chance to use the washroom?"

Up and down the hall I pushed the buggy. It kind of bounced, like that little kids' song about buggy wheels going round and round. Looking at them snuggling down, I decided the twins weren't quite as weird as I had thought. They were still pretty strange though.

When Mrs. Kelly came back they were sound asleep. I wasn't even pushing the buggy anymore. I couldn't. I'd stopped to tuck in one of them and she'd grabbed my finger.

"Thanks, Robyn," said Mrs. Kelly as she pried my finger loose. She pushed the buggy inside the apartment.

Thanks, Robyn. For some reason it made me feel lonely.

5
The Right Place

I couldn't very well go into our apartment and start singing at the top of my lungs and wake the twins again. I lay down on my bed—quietly. I looked up at the ceiling—quietly.

My ceiling is the stippled kind that looks like a moon landscape. When I was little I used to have names for all of the moon craters on my ceiling. The reason I want to be a singer is kind of tied up with those moon craters.

I don't want to go to the moon exactly. I mean, I might want to some day but right now I get feeling pretty weird on the triple-loop roller coaster, so I don't know how I'd feel about blasting off into space. But I do want to do something special like that, something bigger than life. As I said, being the world's greatest singer would fit the bill.

But how could I practise with the twins next door?

I needed a place to sing. A place where it wouldn't bother anyone. A place where the sound could just go on and on. I jumped off the bed, ran out of my apartment, and hurried down the hall.

When you are standing in the cement stairwell of a 15-storey apartment building, the sound can go up and up forever.

"Do, re, mi, fa, so, la, ti, do."

Up and up and up. It didn't sound like a sick cow! It sounded neat. Pretty soon I was singing "Joy to the World" and "Rudolph the Red Nosed Reindeer." It felt great.

Now all I had to do was come up with a song that wasn't about Christmas.

Easy—or at least that's what I thought.

6
Shhhhhh!

Quiet as mice, that's the way my mom said we had to be the next morning. Mr. and Mrs. Kelly had taken the twins to emergency last night. They had something that could easily turn into pneumonia.

"Pneumonia!" I said. "Shouldn't they be in the hospital if they have pneumonia?"

"Not yet," said my mom. "The doctor gave them some medicine. If they can get lots of rest they'll be okay. We can help by being quiet as mice."

Quiet as mice? I was going to be quiet like a rock. Or a slice of pizza. Cartoon characters Number One and Number Two had taken over my place, but I still didn't want them to get pneumonia.

For the next three days I was super quiet. I lip-read TV shows. I practised my piano without pushing down on the piano keys. I didn't slam the doors even once.

I could tell the twins were sick because they still cried a lot, but it wasn't as loud as usual. It was the kind of pathetic sound that drives you crazy. That's why I pushed one of them up and down the hall in the buggy after school each day while Mrs. Kelly fed and settled the other.

Sometimes it was the twin who liked to grab fingers in the buggy, and sometimes it was the other. I could always tell the difference.

While I pushed I sang scales in my head. They kept getting interrupted by something that went "round and round, round and round," but at least I was kind of singing.

After supper I still practised in the stairwell. I was getting pretty sick of scales and Christmas carols. I needed a real song. The trouble is you can't pick up many songs from the TV when you have to lip read. Mom and I weren't turning the radio on at all. I dug out my Walkman and earphones but all it did was squeal in my ear. That was why

I'd stuffed it in the back of my closet in the first place.

"Hey, Snitch—you practising for your big singing debut?" Grant asked me Thursday.

"As a matter of fact I am," I answered. "Thanks for asking."

He smirked at me.

"You lie like a rug," he said.

Finally I asked Marie if we could go to her house and listen to her Celine Dion tapes. It wasn't a success. Celine Dion is a wonderful singer, but she sings way too high for me and I couldn't understand enough of the words to learn a whole song. Besides, Marie plays the tapes so loud it knocks out your eardrums.

That's when I knew the Dragon Lady was my only hope.

7
The Piano Lesson

The Dragon Lady's real name is Mrs. Janvier and she is my piano teacher. She is very strict. She only likes children who practise. She wasn't going to like me much this Saturday, because practising without pushing down on the piano keys doesn't really work very well.

It wasn't a lot of fun sitting in the Dragon Lady's waiting room, thinking about how much she was going to dislike me. It also wasn't much fun because on the other side of the wall some little kid was murdering a song on the piano.

The song was one of the first pieces you get to play with two hands in Mrs. Janvier's classes. I remembered it.

My bonnie lies over the ocean,
My bonnie lies over the sea,
My bonnie lies over the ocean,
Oh, bring back my bonnie to me.

Pretty dumb words, but it's kind of fun to play if it's the first time you get to use two hands at once. And if you're not murdering it. This kid never hit two right notes in a row!

Finally the song stopped and the door opened. It wasn't a kid at all. It was an adult. Adults should not be allowed to take

lessons unless they practise twice as much as kids.

Mrs. Janvier was wearing black. She always wears black. Black is a good colour when you have to listen to songs being murdered the way that adult had just murdered poor old "Bonnie."

I played my scales and pieces. I tried hard not to murder anything. Still, Mrs. Janvier didn't look very friendly. I took a deep breath.

"Mrs. Janvier, could I have a piece with words this week?" I asked. "Just a suggestion."

Mrs. Janvier frowned. She doesn't believe in pieces with words for more advanced students.

"It wouldn't have to be Celine Dion or anything," I said quickly.

"Just something I could sing so I'd practise longer."

She sat very still. I think the episode with "Bonnie" had worn her down.

"Would a song from a Broadway musical be suitable?" she asked.

A Broadway musical! *Annie! Phantom of the Opera!*

But when she brought out the music it was older-looking than either of those. A *lot* older.

Still, the song had a nice melody and I'd heard it before. The words were about someone working in a match factory.

This was going to work after all!

8
Woe is Me!

I felt great as I walked home. As soon as I reached our building I headed for the stairwell, opened up the sheet music and started singing.

Matchmaker, matchmaker,
Make me a match,
Find me a find,
Catch me a catch.

Find me a find? Catch me a catch? What did that mean?

Matchmaker, matchmaker,
I'll bring the veil,
You bring the groom,
Slender and pale …

Veil! Groom! I read further.

The song wasn't about someone in a match factory at all. It was about someone looking for a husband. I couldn't sing a song like that in school! Yuck! How could this happen to me!

I stared at the music so hard I hoped it would disintegrate. I walked out of the stairwell, down the hall, and into my apartment.

"I'm sick," I told my mother. "I may be sick for a long, long time."

I crawled into bed and hid my head under the covers. I didn't want to look up and happen to see any dumb old moonscape in which somebody had named all the craters when they were just a kid.

9
Round and Round

The funny thing about moonscapes is: they don't just exist on ceilings. They exist on the inside of your eyelids even when you squeeze them tight. They exist in your head. They exist inside your ribs where you can't explain things but can still feel them. When you really want to do something, you can't just hide and make it not count anymore. Besides, the Three Gs would call me "snitch" forever. I *had* to have a song.

It was almost suppertime when I gave in. I went into the

living room to dig out the music to old murdered "Bonnie." It wasn't very exciting, but it would have to do. At least I'd make sure I sang it better than "ham hands" had played it.

Mom and Mrs. Kelly were in the living room.

"Good news," said my mom. "Abigail is much better tonight, and Angela is on the mend too."

Abigail and Angela? Hey! I'd forgotten the twins had names!

"Is Abigail the finger-grabber?" I asked.

Mrs. Kelly nodded.

"I thought so," I said. "I hope Angela's well soon too."

"I've brought you something for helping us out," said Mrs. Kelly.

She handed me a small box.

"Actually, I found it this morning at the back of the fridge. I was so busy I forgot about it at Easter," she said.

Inside the box was a beautiful chocolate egg with my name written in pink icing. The twins hadn't replaced me after all! At least not entirely.

"I think it was your singing that pulled them through," said Mrs. Kelly with a little smile. I knew she was joking, but it felt good. Except I didn't understand.

"My singing?" I asked.

"You always sang as you pushed the buggy. Didn't you know? It was kind of humming more than singing—you didn't seem to know many of the words," laughed Mrs. Kelly and then she sang herself. "The wheels on the bus go round and round, round and round, round and round ..."

Those were the words to the song! It wasn't the wheels on the buggy, it was the wheels on the bus. I didn't realize I'd been singing it out loud. And in the other verses the driver says, "Move on back," and the kids go "up and down," and the mothers go "yack yack yack."

I knew the whole song! It was even a song I could act out and make larger than life!

But would everyone laugh at me for singing something I'd learned in pre-school?

10
World's Greatest Singer

When you take a chance, such as blasting off to the moon or singing in front of your class, the way you feel is like you're going to throw up. The palms of my hands got sweaty and cold all at once, and my knees really did feel like jelly. It was kind of fun—if you like living on the edge.

I introduced my performance as "Musical Theatre for Young Children." I figured that would help explain why I was singing a little kid's song.

And then I just sang it—with

all the actions, larger than life. I was especially good at the part about the babies on the bus going "wah wah wah." But what really made it was the verse I made up myself.

"The boys on the bus spit spitballs back, spitballs back, spitballs back."

The Three Gs thought that was pretty good. They even realized I hadn't snitched on them last week.

Mr. Herbert looked like he was actually awake and paying attention.

My best friend, Marie, smiled at me the whole time.

"I really think you're ready to try something by Celine Dion," she said afterward.

If I can figure out the words

and learn to sing really high—
maybe I will.

I hope Abigail and Angela like having a friend who's the world's greatest singer.

Meet five other great kids in the New First Novels Series:

• **Meet Duff the Daring**
in *Duff the Giant Killer*
by Budge Wilson/Illustrated by Kim LaFave
Getting over the chicken pox can be boring, but Duff and Simon find a great way to enjoy themselves — acting out one of their favourite stories, *Jack the Giant Killer*, in the park. In fact, they do it so well the police get into the act.

• **Meet Jan the Curious**
in *Jan's Big Bang*
by Monica Hughes/Illustrated by Carlos Friere
Taking part in the Science Fair is a big deal for Grade Three kids, but Jan and her best friend Sarah are ready for the challenge. Still, finding a safe project isn't easy, and the girls discover that getting ready for the fair can cause a whole lot of trouble.

• **Meet Carrie the Courageous**
in *Go For It, Carrie*
by Lesley Choyce/ Illustrated by Mark Thurman
More than anything else, Carrie wants to roller-blade. Her big brother and his

friend just laugh at her. But Carrie knows she can do it if she just keeps trying. As her friend Gregory tells her, "You can do it, Carrie. Go for it!"

- **Meet Lilly the Bossy**
  in *Lilly to the Rescue*
  by Brenda Bellingham/ Illustrated by Kathy Kaulbach
  Bossy-boots! That's what kids at school start calling Lilly when she gives a lot of advice that's not wanted. Lilly can't help telling people what to do — but how can she keep any of her friends if she always knows better?

- **Meet Morgan the Magician**
  in *Morgan Makes Magic*
  by Ted Staunton/Illustrated by Bill Slavin
  When he's in a tight spot, Morgan tells stories — and most of them stretch the truth, to say the least. But when he tells kids at his new school he can do magic tricks, he really gets in trouble — most of all with the dreaded Aldeen Hummel!

Look for these First Novels!

- ***About Arthur***
  - Arthur Throws a Tantrum
  - Arthur's Dad
  - Arthur's Problem Puppy
- ***About Fred***
  - Fred and the Stinky Cheese
  - Fred's Dream Cat
- ***About the Loonies***
  - Loonie Summer
  - The Loonies Arrive
- ***About Maddie***
  - Maddie in Hospital
  - Maddie Goes to Paris
  - Maddie in Danger
  - Maddie in Goal
  - Maddie Wants Music
  - That's Enough Maddie!
- ***About Mikey***
  - Good For You, Mikey Mite!
  - Mikey Mite Goes to School
  - Mikey Mite's Big Problem
- ***About Mooch***
  - Mooch Forever
  - Hang On, Mooch!
  - Mooch Gets Jealous
  - Mooch and Me
- ***About the Swank Twins***
  - The Swank Prank
  - Swank Talk
- ***About Max***
  - Max the Superhero
